AUTOMNICON:
THE INTERN

by Beth Crane

First published in 2019 by Battle Bird Productions

www.battlebird.productions

www.battlebird.libsyn.com

For more information, get in touch at
battlebirdproductions@gmail.com.

The Intern is dedicated to Hedley Knights. We've spent the last year working like mad on Space Junk and it's been just brilliant.

I also want to say thank you to our Patrons, our lovely Discord and our amazing, supportive group of Audio Drama buddies, as well as everyone who has listened and supported us over the past year. Thank you for taking notice of our little show! It's been really life-changing and we hope to keep working on We Fix Space Junk for years to come!

CHAPTER ONE

She was here. She was finally here. Walking through those hallowed doors.

It might have taken four years of continuous applications, but Astatine was about to begin the first day of her internship at Automnicon.

At approximately the same time, Mr D was about to end his last.

"Lionel… Have him put down."

Lionel, listening on his implant, nodded almost imperceptibly. Mr D, sitting at his desk, was watching him the way a rabbit watches a cat; not in total fear, but in wary silence. Lionel's eyes narrowed and Mr D felt himself shrink.

Mr D stood up, began the long walk from office to bathroom, hoping to rinse the fear from his face. But as he stepped, his quick, neat little footsteps growing in urgency, he heard the quiet, carpeted pad of Lionel's feet behind him.

Lionel never walked fast. His pace was, if anything, languid. But then Lionel was one of nature's stalkers, not sprinters. He never stopped.

Mr D may have thought he was getting away, that the man following him wouldn't catch up, but as he turned a corner, somehow Lionel was there.

The last things that went through Mr D's mind were, in order, strong hands grasping at his collar and his belt, the ding of the lift, the wind rushing past him at a great speed and then, with some finality, the lift itself.

Inside the lift, Astatine jumped at the sudden thump. The lift continued its path upwards.

Lionel was, she decided, going to be a firm friend. He had one of those faces you trusted instinctively. He was there waiting as she exited the lift. He seemed a little surprised to see her, but nonetheless pleased. She introduced herself, they shook hands. His hand was gigantic, smoothed by time and work. Hers felt miniature in his grasp.

He was older, softened in a way you don't often see in offices like these, where everyone has a polished, cold quality. There was something a little sad about him, about the quiet way he walked about in his washed-out grey-black suit. Almost like a monk, padding about silently so as to not get in anyone's way. He directed her to Ms Lamb's office, sat down at one of the two desks outside the door and gestured for her to sit at the other.

The seat was still warm; the technician had presumably been setting it up mere moments before. She opened her eyes wide for the iris scanner. They paused while they registered her for the first time, drying out her eyes and leaving her blinking. After this came the standard tests: the tongue scrape, the fingerprints, blood analysis, genetic analysis, various brain scans and so on. Two hours later, her profile was ready. Lionel was still watching her.

"Ready?"

"Ready."

She stood up and followed him through the door to Ms Lamb's office.

She wasn't sure what she was expecting, but Ms Lamb wasn't it. She was short, attractive, with dark, lively eyes and mismatched eyebrows.

"Astatine. Welcome."

She shuffled a file on her desk. Astatine was surprised to note that she used real paper, which was somewhat of a luxury in the world outside. Lionel left, the door clicking shut behind him.

It was a large office, bigger than any single room she'd ever been inside before. The walls were panelled with fossilised wood; occasional flashes of opalescent colour reflected in it as she passed. Ms Lamb's desk was a semi-circle of dark marble.

"Please. Sit."

She sat down on a short chair that left her looking up at Ms Lamb.

"How are you?"

"Fine. Uh. Glad to be here."

"I know."

"This is all very..." she trailed off, not wanting to say something stupid. Ms Lamb smiled.

"It's a bit much to take in at one glance, isn't it."

"Yes."

Ms Lamb stood, walked across to the wall. She pressed her splayed hand, gently, against it and the wood panelling cleared instantly. Behind it was a wide, curved window, a 180 degree view of the outside. Astatine hesitantly followed her to the window.

It was a long, long, long way down.

"I found your qualifications and your — dedication quite impressive."

Everything Astatine had ever known was below her. The tower she'd grown up in, the school she'd attended, the university… she could see further than she'd ever travelled, than she thought she'd have a chance to travel.

She blinked. For a moment she was dizzy.

"So you're a local girl."

"Yes. I was born here. I was born — there, in fact."

The medical tower was the furthest from the ground she'd ever been before today. It was dwarfed.

"Not many people who grow up in the shadow of our tower want to work here. Fewer get a choice."

"It called to me."

"I see."

Astatine couldn't read her.

"I started out somewhere like this too. A long time ago and a long way away, but... similar. Everywhere you've been, everyone you've interacted with, everything you've done is below us, right now. But, if you're the person I think you are — and I'd be extremely disappointed to find out you weren't — by the time your life is over you'll have travelled far beyond this. The distances will be measured in light years rather than miles. The people you've met will span entire solar systems. You will have seen so much and done so much that this quiet little backwater of a planet will seem almost like a dream."

They were so far above the ground that the people below were less than ants. Tiny, flickering dots on the streets below, barely visible through the clouds of smog that were ever-present.

"I've been watching you for a long time, Astatine. A very long time."

Automnicon's Surveillance Eyes were there on every corner. They tracked the moves of every citizen, made sure that life ran smoothly. They reported traffic, fire, natural disasters and disobedience. Astatine felt warm when she thought of all those eyes watching her. She felt safe.

The fact that Ms Lamb had been behind those eyes watching her too was comforting. That Automnicon and its CEOs cared enough to watch her personally. That Ms Lamb was interested enough.

"Your debt levels are extraordinarily low given your levels of training and experience."

"Well, I knew that if my debt was too high I wouldn't be able to work for Automnicon. Or not in the way that I wanted to, anyway."

"There are always other ways to reduce your debt. But I admire your self-control. I doubt many would be able to do the same. Myself included."

"I'm just… careful."

"So, Astatine. What's your final goal? What do you want from life? And what do you want from us?"

Astatine took a breath.

“The thing I want more than anything?"

"Yes."

"I want to be interested. Entertained. To live a life where things actually happen. The only option I have here is to just continue on the same path forever.

“Since I was born, everyone I know — everyone I've met — has lived in these — these ruts. They're born in these boxes, they travel on the same routes, find a job, find a partner, settle down and then, essentially, they live the rest of their lives waiting to die. I want — no, I need something else. I can't stay here, not like this. This planet — this way of living is strangling me."

Astatine hesitated, self-conscious. She hadn’t quite meant to go that far. She realised her fist was clenched, knuckles white, and released it.

“I... see.”

“I’m — I don't think I'm making myself clear.

What I know is that working for Automnicon, dedicating myself to Automnicon, is the one way to change my life. To get off of this planet, to live a life that isn't just — this, day after day. I'm not a researcher or a scientist. I'm not particularly interesting, I don't have specialities. Not yet. But all I want is to work for you.”

“And what are you willing to sacrifice in exchange?”

“Anything. Anything at all.”

Ms Lamb half-smiled.

"This is everything I've ever wanted."

"I believe you." She blinked, watching Astatine again with an unreadable smile.

Then the moment was over.

"Well, we'll see much more of one another soon, I'm sure. There are big things ahead of you, Astatine. In the meantime, Lionel will find you some work to do."

CHAPTER TWO

"We'll start with filing."

"Really?"

"We need to know what you're capable of."

"I've done filing before. I've done a hell of a lot of it."

She felt the walls closing in around her. If Automnicon was just going to be more of the same, then what was the point? Why dedicate herself to it, why risk her relationships with her family and friends if all she was going to do was more soul-crushing admin?

Lionel flared his nostrils, gave the tiniest hint of a smile.

"Come on. Follow me."

She followed Lionel through the double doors and as he padded along the long, carpeted corridor. They went downwards in a slow, gradual spiral. The air was getting colder, drier; Astatine felt the itching of a cough in her throat.

After long minutes of walking, in front of them, finally, were the double doors of the filing department.

Why there was a physical filing system at all, Astatine was unsure; as far as she knew, Automnicon's information was available across the whole galaxy. It operated as one entity across the known universe, which was getting bigger every day.

Passing through the double doors, they arrived in a room full of climbing gear, harnesses and ropes. Lionel stopped, sized her up for a minute then handed her a harness. He then pulled his own, labelled, from a locker.

She hadn't quite realised the size of Lionel. Sure, he was tall, but his slightly baggy suit concealed broad shoulders and wide, powerful arms. She wondered exactly what he'd done to earn his role as Ms Lamb's personal secretary. Presumably it wasn't his telephone manner.

He pulled his harness on and she did the same, buckling it tight around her waist and shoulders. She followed him, hesitantly, into the next room.

It turned out to be a circular industrial lift, open-topped. Lionel clipped himself into a ring on the safety rail and she copied him with growing apprehension. Then he picked up the control box, pressed the green button.

With a metallic groan, the lift descended.

And descended.

And descended.

The filing chamber was a tube thirty feet across, packed wall-to-wall with files. Every ten feet their descent activated another ring of lights; as far as Astatine could see, the chamber went on for miles, the bottom of the room lost in darkness.

Each file was clipped into its shelf to avoid its permanent loss at the bottom of the shaft; Astatine shivered to think about what might be down there.

She wished she'd worn something thicker than her suit. It had seemed a good, sturdy purchase at the time; something passed down with minimal wear to the thrift stores by someone who'd decided to upgrade, a real find. But the thin fabric was not the most practical for this cold, sterile atmosphere.

"This is Automnicon's central filing system. The soul of the company. Everything that Automnicon has ever done or has ever intended to do is stored here."

He took a deep, satisfied breath.

"This is my favourite room in the whole building. I find it… soothing. Like Automnicon is taking care of everything."

"So why is everything stored here like this?"

"It's data. The whole of Automnicon runs on data. It's a cliche, but knowledge is power. In the wrong hands — or the right ones — it can lead to major changes. Overthrow governments. Destroy or create despots. Trigger assassinations, revolutions, or just bolster obedience.

And sometimes, what we need most of all is for that data to disappear. Sometimes temporarily, sometimes permanently. But we keep a record of it, because without the full facts, we don't have the full picture.

Everything Automnicon has ever learned is stored here.

These drives are truly individual. Non-networked, inaccessible to anyone outside of the person who holds the physical copy. A lot of them are obsolete, but you never know when it's worth letting a little bit of data... resurface. Whether we're trying to drum up support, smooth things over between battling neighbours or begin a war.

We'll do something more interesting with them eventually, but for now we just need you to fetch the files on the list."

"Doesn't that make everything here confidential? Why are you letting me see all this?"

"You were thoroughly vetted."

"But — "

"Very thoroughly. You've been monitored by statisticians, behavioral analysts, psychiatrists, management specialists…"

"For an internship?"

He laughed. "Well. Close enough."

"Shouldn't we be wearing helmets?"

Lionel blinked.

"If you fall, a helmet isn't going to do you any good."

Eventually the lift stopped with a juddering thunk. Astatine realised she was clinging on to the railing. She let go, self-conscious.

In front of them was a narrow walkway, less than a foot wide, no barriers on either side; little more than a metal gangplank.

"This is your first stop."

She gulped.

"You can stay clipped into the safety rail until you reach the wall, then I'll unclip you and you can attach yourself to one of the abseil lines."

Every four or five feet around the wall was a rope on a set of pulleys with carabiners at regular intervals. She looked from the lift to the wall and felt her heart pound in her chest. How many interns had they lost in here? What was waiting at the bottom? Would they even find her if she fell?

"The abseil lines are geared. They shouldn't move more than, say, ten to twenty feet per second; slow enough for you to catch hold of the wall if you're falling. If you're lucky. If you aren't... Well. Be lucky."

She took a deep breath, edged herself out along the gangplank. When she reached the wall, she clung on tight, her hands painful from the pressure. Looking back at Lionel she saw another hint of a smile.

"Well done."

He unclipped her and she clipped herself into the abseil rail.

"Alright, then. Fetch me the file on Garten, Ned. Number 22,539,B."

Looking around her, she gradually deciphered the filing system. The wall was broken into 26 segments, lettered A-Z; they were at level 539, which meant that Ned Garten's file was number 22 in section B. She held her breath as she moved from abseil rope to abseil rope until she reached section B, then ran her fingers along the files until she found number 22. There it was. Ned Garten.

She exhaled, let herself relax for a moment, then gradually worked her way back round to Lionel.

The file was a clear perspex panel, about the size of a sheet of paper. The name was etched on the edge but the rest of it was blank. When she handed it to Lionel, he pressed his finger to the edge and, briefly, the panel was filled with densely-packed, layered text. He smiled, placed it by his feet and gave her another file to pull.

A few hours later, although her whole body ached, she'd started to get the hang of it. Rather than clinging tight to the wall, she found herself leaping from shelf to shelf. She pulled file after file until Lionel's stack was knee high.

The next name on the list was close to her. Not wanting the hassle of clipping on to the next rope, she leaned across, her fingers brushing the next file. Just an inch further…

And then she was falling. And falling. She battered against the shelves, tried to catch hold but she seemed to be travelling faster with every foot she fell. She looked up as she fell into the darkness. And then, suddenly, she came to a jarring stop, bouncing on her rope. Above her, Lionel braced himself against the shelf, rope wrapped around and around his arm. He leaned back, gradually dragged her back up. She clawed her way back onto the lift platform, gulping down air.

Lionel just smiled.

He'd been expecting her to fall, she thought.

Then, with a start, she realised that his safety rope wasn't clipped on to anything. He'd leapt out of the lift to catch her without anything but his own balance to rely on.

The rest of the afternoon was a bit of a blur. She pulled more files, making sure she was safe this time. She didn't slip again; she didn't take any chances.

The stack of files beside Lionel grew higher and higher until he ticked off the last name. Finally he beckoned her back on to the platform and she gratefully returned.

"You did well today. I was expecting you to need more of a break after you fell."

"I didn't know that was an option."

"It wasn't."

He pressed the button and the lift travelled upwards. He smiled and Astatine wondered exactly what he'd meant.

It was only as she was taking off her harness that Astatine realised she was soaked through with sweat. Her suit and hair were both dripping.

"Here." Lionel handed her a bottle of water and a bar of something sweet, both of which she inhaled within moments. "We missed lunch."

"So what do you want me to do next?"

"Go home. Get some rest. You'll need it."

"Really?"

"We've got a lot to do tomorrow."

She looked at her watch, realised it was late, far later than she thought. The trains would still be busy but at least there'd be less of a wait on the platforms. And she would probably get at least a little space on the way home, sodden with sweat as she was.

CHAPTER THREE

Ms Lamb sat cross-legged on her desk, watching the sunlight play on the pollution that shadowed the city. Occasionally a cloud would ignite for a moment with a flash of flame then flicker out into fine, black dust.

The door opened and Lionel padded silently in.

"How did she do?"

"She fell around a quarter of the way in, but that was more due to over-eagerness than anything else. I think she's going to become quite the climber."

He dropped the files onto her desk.

"Well, that's a good start, at least."

"Tomorrow's going to be a little harder. She's not worked with weaponry before. I'm not entirely sure how she'll react."

She'll do fine. I'm certain of it."

He paused, looked at her.

You like this one, don't you?"

he hesitated.

"I don't know what you're talking about."

"Nothing wrong with that. It's been a long time."

"Lionel — " She shot him a warning look.

He shrugged.

She went back to watching the clouds.

Astatine's journey home was a blur. The train was the same as it had always been, everyone wedged shoulder-to-shoulder. There had been seats on these trains once, apparently, but they'd been removed to make way for the sheer crush of people.

Travelling on the trains was an art, even outside of rush hour; you had to calculate the exact right point to stand or you'd be shoved off of the train too early or trapped on until far, far too late. Those new to the transport system could frequently be found wedged in odd corners of the train right to the end of the line. But Astatine had practiced this journey so many times, even before she'd been accepted for her internship.

She got off at Dallas Station and began the long trek to her building. The rain was starting to fall again, and the pollution was bad today; the water hissed and smoked as it hit the garbage lying in the street. The perspex-roofed walkways were more crowded than usual; after all, nobody wanted to risk chemical burns (and the resulting medical bills).

Astatine lived on the outskirts of the city. As her peers had moved into bigger, more expensive spaces, she'd stayed in the one-room flat she'd rented since she was a student. It wasn't a glamorous space but it was entirely tolerable. Eighteen floors up, which kept her fit, at least. There had been surprising amount of fitness trials to pass before she'd been accepted for her internship.

She stopped off at the commissary on floor sixteen, ostensibly to pick up her food parcels for the week but actually to see Rita.

She'd been eating the same meal every evening for the past four years. It could only really be described as food by the fact that it contained the necessary nutrients to sustain human life, but it was the most cost-effective way to not die of starvation.

She had an ongoing flirtation of sorts with Rita, who'd run the commissary as long as Astatine had lived in the building. She occasionally fantasised about going further than whatever it was that had been gradually building between them, but there was always something that stood in her way.

Rita was tall, with hair that fell in loose curls around her face. She didn't seem to have aged in all the years that Astatine had known her, and her amusement at her bare-bones choice of nutrition didn't seem to have ceased. From time to time, Astatine would find extra packets of flavouring slipped in with her regular meals.

"Astatine! So good to see you. The usual?" Her tone, as always, was warm and welcoming. It was part of coming home.

Rita's hand brushed hers as she handed over the food parcel and she let her hand linger. Their eyes met. Maybe today. She always thought it. Maybe today.

"You're late, were you..."

Rita's eyes flickered downwards. Her face paled, her mouth drew in tight. She withdrew her hands, wiped them on her apron like she'd touched something slimy. She shoved Astatine's parcel across the counter and turned away, almost nauseous.

Astatine picked up her parcel and walked away. She'd forgotten to take her lanyard off.

Joining Automnicon was a quick way to lose friends. Since the corporation had implanted themselves in the city a century before, they had entirely overrun the local economy. Nobody knew why exactly they'd chosen to build their vast complex on an obscure planet on the outskirts of nowhere, but they had quickly become the only real industry, beyond the usual.

While her family and friends feared and loathed Automnicon by turns, Astatine had seen them as something else entirely; a way to escape. The only way to escape.

Before Automnicon, the planet had been an obscure settler's outpost, a place established and populated exclusively by the descendents of a single human ark ship. Terraforming had gone poorly; the few crops that they'd managed to grow had a salty, almost chlorinated taste to them and without a constant stream of vitamin supplements the population would have been dead of malnutrition within a decade. The atmosphere was mostly breathable, although the pollution that was the unfortunate byproduct of human civilisation had caused toxic clouds of smog to linger in the skies above the city. All in all, it was a dull, grey place, with nothing that wasn't functional and little that was beautiful.

The humans of the planet made do.

But the arrival of Automnicon had opened up the planet to whole new peoples, whole new species. While unpopular, even their harshest critics had to admit that they'd changed the face of the planet. They'd changed the face of the whole galaxy. And someday they would take her off-world, take her to new and exciting places.

And Rita would stay behind. She'd marry another woman and they'd grow old and grey together, running the commissary. And that wasn't the life that Astatine wanted.

She walked up the final few flights of stairs and along the corridor on to her apartment. She unlocked her front door, sat on her bed and opened the fridge. Her apartment, like all of the apartments in the building and most of the apartments in that zone, was approximately seven feet by four, with a two by four wetroom behind a sliding door. The decor was chipped vinyl and water-stained stainless steel.

She sat on her bed, pulled a bowl out of the cupboard and tipped the powder that made up that night's meal into it. She topped it up with boiling water from the kettletap, let the water dissolve most of the powder then stirred it, left it to set. After five minutes the meal had rehydrated.

Automni-meals. All of the nutrients you require with nothing superfluous. She was on Meal Type B, which was for High Activity Roles. She'd switched from the cheaper Type C, Sedentary Roles, as soon as she'd sent in her first application to Automnicon. She'd been surprised at quite how much worse it had tasted, given that the thin gruel of Type C was a virtually flavourless, gritty paste with an unpleasant tang, but she'd felt an increase in energy and focus within a week.

She scraped up the last of it then dumped her spoon and bowl in the dishwashing chute. A replacement would be delivered within a few minutes, shiny and worn smooth from a hundred thousand washes.

Her shoulder ached and her knees were bruised where she'd crashed against the shelves. She'd feel rough as hell in the morning and, she realised, her suit needed patching where she'd caught it on a shelf.

She sank back onto her bed, smiling. She'd made it. Finally.

She was finally there.

CHAPTER FOUR

She didn't see much of Ms Lamb in the week that followed, although she thought that perhaps the Surveillance Eyes were a bit more attentive than usual. A few times she caught herself smiling directly at them, wondering if Ms Lamb was watching.

It was silly and sycophantic, she knew, but there was something magnetic about Ms Lamb. Something that made it hard to get her off of her mind.

"She sounds like a nightmare. Exactly your type."

Juna stretched out on Astatine's bed as Astatine brushed her teeth. Juna had arrived on her doorstep two days after Astatine had begun her internship. She was bedraggled and knackered as usual. Juna was one of those people who enjoyed themselves a little too much, drank too deeply, stared too intently. Sometimes she'd crash back down and occasionally she'd take everyone around her with her.

These days she'd drop in and out of her friends' lives like a feral cat. She'd been missing for a few months but she usually found her way back.

She was usually bright, bubbly, but right now her eyes were deep set in her sockets, lined with wrinkles that hadn't been there last time. It had only been a few months since Astatine had seen her last but they'd clearly been hard on her. She couldn't keep her eyes focused on any one thing.

Juna had been one of the first EL-8 addicts. She still had the ports in the back of her neck, although they looked like they'd mostly healed up. A jolt of very specific electricity right to the pleasure points of the brain. It sounded like a good idea, a non-chemical high, but it quickly created scar ring; overuse made it impossible to feel pleasure from much else.

"I knew that thing with — whatsername, the shop girl — wouldn't work out. She's just too nice for you. You like them a bit more — aggressive. Powerful."

"Okay, can we not? She's my boss and I've got to work with her."

"Nothing wrong with a bit of office romance. I've had a few in my time."

"Yeah, and how did that work out for you?"

Juna shrugged and Astatine noticed a new set of scars across her shoulder.

"Come on. Let's go out. Out out."

"That's a really bad idea."

"Where's your sense of adventure?"

"Going out isn't an adventure, it's just an accident waiting to happen. Can't we just have a quiet night?"

"Oh come on. It's been ages. Just me and you. Girls' night out."

Astatine shrugged.

"Fine. How bad can it be?"

The answer, it emerged, was very, very bad.

Juna had stuck around long enough for Astatine to get uncomfortably drunk and then, without warning, she'd vanished, along with Astatine's bag, all of her money and her comms. After half an hour of searching, Astatine had given up and begun the long walk home.

She'd not walked home in a long time. The skies stayed dry but the wind whistled uncomfortably through the streets, chilling her to the core and tangling her hair across her face. She could still use the emergency keysafe to get into her flat, so that was something at least. The rest she'd have to deal with the next day.

The sky was light by the time she'd rounded the corner. She made her way up in the lift (a rarity for her) and, an hour before she was due to leave, she made it to her front door. Just as she was approaching, it swung wide and a man, tall, dark and reeking of last night's booze, slipped out and headed directly for the stairs, avoiding eye contact.

Inside, Juna was lying sprawled across the bed.

"Seriously?"

"What?"

"What in Bruce's name did you do last night?"

"Oh. I wasn't feeling well, so I went home." Her voice was slurred, drowsy.

"And that was…?"

"Karl. I think? He helped me home. He was... nice."

"Sure he was."

"I'm sorry."

"I had to walk."

Juna looked up at her, her eyes round and sad.

"I said I'm sorry."

"Get out of my way. I need to shower."

She picked up her bag, keys and comms device still safely inside, dressed briskly and left for work, leaving Juna still curled up in bed. Astatine had other things to worry about.

As the door clicked shut, Juna sat up, no longer feigning a hangover. She leaned over, looked at her comms. A clone of Astatine's screen looked back at her.

CHAPTER FIVE

"So, how do you feel your first week has gone?"

Astatine, hangover still ringing in her head, sank into the chair and smiled, wearily. Ms Lamb watched her, her fingers steepled and her head to one side like a cat's. Her eyes were fixed on her, intently.

"It's gone well. I think." She was hesitant; there had been problems here and there but overall it had been positive.

The weapons training had been first. She'd never used any kind of weapon in her life, but there was something satisfying about the point-and-click nature of it. She'd taken a while to get used to it, but by the end of the day she was managing to keep her eyes open when she fired. At some point soon she'd presumably start hitting the target.

This was followed by some kind of martial art. Why an intern needed training in unarmed combat she really wasn't sure, but nonetheless she embraced it. She had a couple of cuts that probably wouldn't scar too badly to show for it, but she'd done quite well by the end of the day.

Apparently she was enrolled in both for the rest of the year.

Later in the week she'd moved onto surveillance, with a little light digital intrusion. Although it wouldn't be part of her day to day activities, Lionel had explained, it was important for her to have an overview of what the different departments did. She found it fascinating watching the citizens of the city, and the additional access that Automnicon had to their digital world made it doubly interesting.

She didn't have to wonder what the man on the phone was so worried about when with a swipe she could hear both sides of the conversation. She knew exactly why the grim-faced woman was leaving the health centre with such trepidation. Every human had a story and Automnicon wanted to know them all. Astatine wanted to know them all.

After surveillance she'd gone into supplies. An organisation the size of Automnicon went through a truly colossal quantity of disposable stock on a day-to-day basis; their building had a weekly standing order for more bullets and explosives than the average despot's private army. And their real food order was truly astounding; for someone whose nutritional intake was almost solely in the form of rehydrated powders, the fact that Automnicon spent the average employee's monthly wage just on fresh tomatoes every day was gobsmacking.

Ms Lamb looked at her. "You've been coping admirably with everything we've thrown at you. Not that I expected less."

Astatine felt her stomach turn a little; last night's drinks were making themselves known again.

"Really?"

"Well, we've been taking a special interest in you for… quite some time. Not every intern lives up to their potential." Ms Lamb paused a moment, looked at her closely. "Would you like a glass of water?"

"Oh. I — "

"Oh, we know." She smiled. "Nothing wrong with a night off. Just don't let your guard down."

"Were you — "

"Someone always is."

"So how long have you been — watching — me?"

"Me personally or Automnicon in general? I can't speak for Automnicon, but I've been — aware of you, at least, for four, maybe five years?"

"But I applied so many times!"

"And you were an excellent candidate."

"I didn't even start applying til — " Astatine tried to work it out. She'd been applying to Automnicon for so long that she'd lost track.

'Oh, you were flagged at quite an early age."

'But — "

'You were perfectly — fine, the first time. But we were curious as to wheth-er you could improve, given… motivation. Your second application showed hat you could, and your third…

Well. Let's say you were very nearly here this time last year. But I wanted to et you mature a little. Like wine."

Astatine nodded. Not that wine was something she'd come across, but she upposed the analogy made sense.

"But those who wait long enough are rewarded. And now, here you are."

Ms Lamb shifted in her seat, her eyes intent on her.

"As intern to one of Automnicon's CEOs, obviously you'll be working harder and for longer hours. Eventually you can expect a better paid position, although obviously you won't be paid until you are officially employed with us. But special low-interest loans are available to our most talented interns."

"I'm... reluctant to take out a loan."

"I know. I'm afraid that there are times at which it is necessary to further yourself. But I will bear it in mind, of course."

Astatine shrank back, embarrassed. Ms Lamb stood, walked around the desk towards her. Even seated, Astatine was the same height as her.

She had a scent that Astatine couldn't quite place. A combination of citrus and engine oil.

"Being reserved with money is nothing to be ashamed of. But make sure your reservations don't actively harm your chances of employment. Especially if you want to stay with us."

"I do. More than anything."

"I'm glad. We just have one final task that we need you to do before we can bring you into the team."

Ms Lamb rested her hand on Astatine's shoulder. It was soft, unexpectedly warm.

"What do you want me to do?"

CHAPTER SIX

Astatine and Juna sat across from one another at The Spoon, the ghost of a pub that had once been their regular haunt. Frederik, the barman, was still there, but most of the regulars were not. He still remembered their usual orders, still undercharged them.

It was more expensive than Astatine was comfortable with, but she couldn't have Meal Plan B for every meal and the atmosphere in the tiny flat was starting to get oppressively apologetic.

"How did the rest of your week go?"

Juna looked up at her, smiled wearily. They'd do a bit of small talk and then things would get back to normal again.

"Really well. Tiring, but... well."

"Spent much more time with Ms Lamb?"

"Not — really. But I had a review with her yesterday and it went really well, so... we'll see."

"This is what you wanted, right?"

"Yeah."

"I never got my head around why that was the job for you. You've always been so… determined."

"It's what I want to do. It's what I've always wanted. But..."

"But what?"

"I'm worried I'm not up to it."

"Can you talk about it?"

"Not really. Most of it's classified."

"Of course it is."

Astatine pushed her plate away, drained her drink in one gulp. Frederik came over with their bill and Astatine paid.

"Are you sure?"

"It's fine. I've budgeted for it."

Juna laughed, and for a moment she seemed her old self.

"Alright then."

"Want to take a walk? Looks like the rain's stopped."

They walked for what felt like hours. The temperature dropped but they didn't hurry; the sky was dry so they had nothing to flee from and nothing to head towards. Walking faster just meant they'd be home, be sitting in silence sooner. Speaking was easier when they were walking, and it had been far too long long since they'd last talked properly.

"Is it everything you wanted it to be?"

“Yeah. But it’s been hard. Really hard. Far harder than I expected. And I’ve got my last test coming up and it’s all a lot to think about. I’m worried that maybe I should just… not do it.”

“Astatine. Since we've known each other, what's been the one constant?"

"I..."

"You've always wanted to work for Automnicon. And somehow, despite that, our friendship has survived. This, for some strange, unknown reason, is what you want to do with your life."

"It is."

"There are hurdles in every... dream career, even if to everyone else this seems more like a nightmare. But I believe in you. You can do it. You can do anything."

She turned to Astatine, her eyes serious.

"Even if I hate what you become. You can do it."

The sun began to turn the night sky pale. Seagulls cawed harshly in the morning light and the sour, salt smell of the sea filled their nostrils. They looked out over the docks, over the black sludge of the sea.

Juna squeezed her shoulder, her eyes warm.

“Don't worry. You'll ace it. You have it in you. You know you do.”

Astatine smiled back.

“Thank you. You’ve… really helped.”

The Surveillance Eyes had been watching other things for some time. Astatine had noticed them turning their cameras away during their walk. As if they knew.

She was cleaning Juna's blood off of her hands when she heard footsteps.

"Well done, Astatine."

Ms Lamb was standing behind her. She didn't know how long she'd been watching.

Astatine heaved the body into the harbour. The acid would melt it into little more than toxic gunk in a couple of hours. Then, suddenly dizzy, she fell to her hands and knees, retched until there was nothing left but bile.

CHAPTER SEVEN

She stayed there on her hands and knees for what felt like hours. Above her, the skies opened and acrid rain began to fall. Too long outdoors and it would burn right through her skin. For a minute she wondered about just letting it.

Ms Lamb seemed unaffected. "It had to happen one way or another."

Astatine took a deep breath, felt the acid rise in her throat once more. She couldn't speak.

'She didn't see it coming."

'I think she did."

Ms Lamb shrugged. "Well, it was a clean job. That's all you can ask for really."

Yeah."

Ms Lamb bent down and took her elbow in her hand. She helped her to her feet, helped her stumble out of the rain. Already the cheap fabric of her jacket was splintering like wet tissue paper.

You passed."

Yes."

"You're shaking."

"I know."

"Come on."

The rain picked up as they made it back under cover.

Astatine took a deep breath, tried flippancy and failed. "What are you doing in this part of the town? Doesn't strike me as a particularly friendly place for someone like you."

"I can look after myself. Have you been drinking?"

"Maybe a little. Needed the courage."

"You need something to eat."

"How long have you been following me?"

"Long enough."

They sat down at a concrete table outside a kerbside diner. The rain spattered heavily now. Nobody would be looking for bodies in this kind of weather. Not that anybody would be looking for Juna anyway.

Ms Lamb scanned her card — no, her ring finger — against the table's serving sensor. Astatine looked closer at Ms Lamb's hand. What she'd thought was a ring was a broad metal joint, polished to the point of brilliance. The finger above it, although relatively realistic, was artificial.

"You like it? I'm considered a little… old-fashioned. My colleagues might be happy to have clones grown for replacement parts but I've always preferred the idea of a prosthetic as an upgrade."

She flicked her finger open, revealing a swiss army knife's worth of gadgets. After a moment it was gone again, back to uncanny-valley normality.

She tapped the button on top of the table's screen for attention from the diner's AI.

"Coffee. See my log for how I like it."

The AI unit blooped hesitantly. "Are — are you sure? The file seems — corrupted."

"Oh no, that's correct. Go on."

"I'll have the same," Astatine added.

"Are you sure? You'll regret it. Oh, and bring us — two mega-meals. The real-food ones, not the reformed."

Astatine looked at her. "I'm not scared of a strong coffee."

"It's not exactly strong coffee. Honestly, it's barely coffee. But I developed a taste for it when I was younger and now… well, I don't get the same kick out of anything else."

Two rusted metal cups clanked onto the table, followed by a whooshing, steaming splutter as the coffee was dispensed.

"Your — your beverages. Ma'am."

"They aren't legally permitted to call it coffee." Ms Lamb took a long sip, sighed with pleasure and put the cup down. "Perfect. Thank you."

The AI bipped nervously again then went silent.

The beverage was a slightly green-tinted brown, and was almost too insubstantial to be called a liquid. Peculiar oily patterns danced upon and above the surface. Astatine raised the cup, hesitantly, Ms Lamb watching with her eyebrows raised.

She took a sip. The first thing that she felt was a sharp pain in her teeth. The not-coffee burned in her throat. She felt her tastebuds buzzing and expiring in protest. It mixed with the acid brewing in her stomach and she felt sick, sicker than she had before.

"Told you so." Ms Lamb grinned in a way she hadn't seen before. "My first ship had a defective drinks dispenser and I couldn't afford to get it replaced. But I was so desperate for anything resembling coffee that I drank it anyway. It took me three years to get used to this stuff. Excessive consumption is — not advisable."

She tipped Astatine's cup into hers with a sizzle and ordered her a plain black coffee. It came in an ordinary ceramic mug which clinked onto the counter.

"Most places around here keep a couple of rusted mugs just for me. It's part of the chemical reaction. And I tip well."

She took Astatine's coffee from the dispenser, passed it along the table. Her fingers lingered on the cup as Astatine took it. It was refreshingly ordinary.

"To your future."

"And to Automnicon." And to Juna, she added silently. Sorry.

They clinked their mugs together as their food came. Not that she could eat it; she hesitantly pushed beans around her plate while Ms Lamb tucked in. Eventually she managed a slice of dried toast.

The flat was quiet when she returned. Late at night she thought she heard Juna get up to use the bathroom, but it was just people moving around in the other apartments.

There were strands of her hair everywhere, left there as if she was forcing Astatine to remember her. Every time was a kick in the stomach. She'd already thrown up more times than she could count.

She took another antacid, hoped her stomach would settle soon and tried to sleep. Eventually she drifted off into a world of putrid oceans, dissolving mermaids and long, ensnaring strands of hair.

CHAPTER EIGHT

Three weeks later and she'd regained her ability both to sleep and digest food. She wasn't seeing Juna out of the corner of her eye any more and she'd stopped hearing her voice. The hairs, as she'd found them, she'd banished to the waste disposal, along with the scant possessions Juna had left scattered about the place. Presumably she'd moved some of her things out; she'd found no ID, no money, no comms. Unless they'd been on her body.

She sat at her computer, rubbing a bruise from yesterday's training. Today was a quiet day; she'd spent it tapping into conversations and Automnicon's Surveillance Eyes. Once or twice she thought she'd spotted the man who'd snuck out of her apartment after his tryst with Juna. But it was never him, and she'd only ever had a glance at his face anyway.

She looked up, smiled as Ms Lamb approached.

Ms Lamb smiled broadly. "Go home and pack your bags. You're moving. Lionel will be with you at eight."

"My apartment is fine. Really. I can't afford — "

"It's a compulsory upgrade. And don't worry. It's being paid for."

About the only element of her apartment building that she was still attached to was Rita, and they were no longer talking. So, swallowing her trepidation, she went home and packed up everything she owned into a small rucksack.

She noticed a last remaining hair stuck into the velcro of her bag. She unwound it slowly then, rather than put it into the waste disposal as she usually did, she wound it up into a tiny coil, put it into an envelope.

It was hard to leave Juna behind entirely.

There were a lot of elements that she'd come to think of as hers that were actually built into the room. The kettle tap, the endlessly renewing retractable duvet, even the electric toothbrush were part of the building, not things she could pack up and take with her.

She wondered whether she should bid farewell to Rita, but as she'd passed the commissary on the way up she'd caught her eye and Rita had almost snarled, the disgust clear on her face. So that was a no. She seemed to have moved on, anyhow, exchanging lingering glances with the grey-haired girl from the floor below. Perhaps she'd always done that, Astatine didn't know.

At eight p.m., Lionel knocked on her door. She opened it and he peered in, a little surprised at the sheer lack of scale. Suddenly she felt self-conscious, defensive of the place she'd spent so much time in over the past decade. It was small, and strange, but it was hers. But now it was hers no longer.

Onward to newer, brighter things.

CHAPTER NINE

The front door was green. It was a silly thing, but Astatine had never seen a front door that wasn't painted one of the four standard shades of grey. It was alien, something ordinary but not quite right.

It opened, and Ms Lamb stood in the doorway.

"Welcome home!"

Astatine smiled nervously, walked inside. Ms Lamb shut the door behind her. Lionel had, apparently, gone off somewhere else.

The apartment was big. Bigger than any apartment Astatine had ever been in. There was a screen on one wall, a sofa — an actual sofa. A kitchen area with a real fridge and a stove (not that she really knew how to use one.) A bed that was three times the width of her old one.

There was even a separate bathroom with an actual bath. She didn't think baths existed outside of books any more.

There were a few more surprises around the place. Crockery, some of it second-hand. The wardrobe was half-full of clothes, mostly mens' shirts and corporate wear. There were soap and toiletries in the bathroom, dried and tinned food in the cupboards.

"Whose is all of this stuff?"

"Oh, don't worry about it. Sometimes people just leave things behind when they move in a hurry. Keep anything you want, get rid of the rest."

A chime rang out and Astatine jumped.

"That's the doorbell. I guess the previous tenant was a bit of a traditionalist."

Lionel opened the door, carried in a large paper bag. It clinked as he set it down with the promise of glass bottles. The air was suddenly rich with the scent of chow mein. He set it down on the table, began decanting the contents.

Ms Lamb kicked off her shoes and sat cross-legged on the sofa. Her toes glinted silver through slightly sheer socks.

Astatine sat down beside her, hesitantly, as Lionel ferried across takeaway cartons.

"I had to guess what you'd like, so I went with something fairly ordinary. This place does the best food though. Bruce knows why they stayed on-world but I'm glad they did."

Astatine opened the box. She hadn't realised quite how hungry she was until that moment.

A good meal and several strong beers later, Astatine found herself in the middle of a heated discussion about the business of remade cinema when they all realised that it was getting late. Ms Lamb sighed and she and Lionel both stood up, started going through the motions of getting ready to leave.

"Do you — want to stay? I have room. Obviously."

Ms Lamb laughed. “No, I’ve got somewhere else to be. Relax. Get used to the place. You’ve probably got some unpacking to do. Come in a little later tomorrow.”

As Lionel closed the door behind them, the sound echoed around the room. Astatine shivered. She’d never been alone in a space this big before.

She got undressed, a little tipsy, and crawled into the bed. The wide expanse of space above her was troubling, like being naked under the stars.

After twenty minutes of trying to ignore the exposure, Astatine got up again. She pushed the bed into the corner of the room and surrounded it with chairs from the kitchen area — four chairs! What person needs four whole chairs?

She draped a blanket across the top, secured it with cable ties. Finally she pulled the big cushions off of the sofa and pushed them up against the wall, making the space inside more compact, less terrifyingly open.

In her blanket fort, protected from the expanse of space outside, Astatine snored, softly.

In Astatine’s old apartment, Ms Lamb and Lionel tore the room apart, until finally Lionel held up a comms device; the one Juna had cloned from Astatine.

He dropped it to the ground and stamped it flat.

CHAPTER TEN

For Astatine, the weeks following on from the move were a bit of a blur. She spent her time filing and training. She'd taken to joining Ms Lamb at the gym; even there she wore a kind of business suit, although one a little more suited to strenuous exercise. Astatine was starting to match her in speed and strength, despite Ms Lamb's technological advantages.

She still hadn't gotten used to the size of her apartment, although her blanket fort had gotten slightly bigger. She now had room to curl up in a foetal position if she wanted to instead of lying perfectly straight.

One evening she attempted to cook an egg, and for the most part she succeeded. It took her three attempts before she realised that she needed to take the shell off before eating, although the extra calcium presumably did her some good.

There was no commissary here, but fresh food seemed to show up in her flat at fairly regular intervals and, she discovered through some trial and error, the majority of it could be eaten raw. She started staying later at the office, helping Ms Lamb and Lionel with this and that. All in all, life was relatively good. She looked forward to work, looked forward to the short walk in, even looked forward to the awkward small talk with the receptionist who greeted her each day.

But then, one day, something was wrong.

Astatine had grown accustomed to her pass taking her straight up to the top floor, almost to the door of Ms Lamb's office. Today it bleeped, the light flashed red and instead it deposited her five floors below. Slowly she climbed the stairs.

The office was gone. There was only a ghost of Ms Lamb's name on the door. Astatine and Lionel's desks had been polished up and now contained a virtually identical pair of incredibly pale secretaries, their eyes blank and unfriendly.

Astatine backed off. She went down to the front desk, trying to conceal her the growing panic.

"What's happened to Ms Lamb?"

The receptionist looked at her, blankly.

"Who?"

"Ms Lamb. The CEO. About this tall, brown eyes, curly hair — " she looked at the receptionist again, noticing the fear in their eyes that she hadn't noticed before. A look of warning.

"I — don't know about her. Mr King has always been the CEO here."

They widened their eyes again, nodded slowly. She nodded back.

"How… strange of me. To forget our CEO. Perhaps I'm getting sick."

"Maybe you should go home."

"I — will." She looked back at them.

"Take care of yourself, Astatine."

The door closed behind her as she left. She'd gone more than a mile before she realised that she was running at full speed. Where, she wasn't sure.

She took a deep breath and turned towards home.

CHAPTER ELEVEN

She was still able to enter her residential building; clearly she hadn't had her access revoked. The lift set off upwards like it always did.

She looked down at the lift floor, noticed a single red spot. A dark red bead of liquid.

She felt her breath catch in her chest. She reached down to touch it, to see if it was what she thought it was, but then the lift pinged and the doors slid open.

There was more blood in the hallway. The occasional drip became regular, then got heavier and heavier as she reached her front door, which swung open as she touched it. Inside, the floor was smeared, sticky with it. Bloody clothes lay in a trail towards her bathroom.

Astatine approached the door, nudged it open.

Ms Lamb was lying in her bath. Most of the blood seemed to have come from the cut on her head, which still oozed a dark trail through her hair. There was a bullet hole in her shoulder that had also slowed to a trickle.

Her eyes were closed, her face spattered and bruised. Astatine stepped closer, reached out to touch her, then stopped.

Ms Lamb's eyes flickered open and she looked towards Astatine with a weary half-smile.

“Are you alright?”

“What? Oh, nothing wrong with me our technicians can’t fix.” Ms Lamb tensed, winced.

“What do you need me to do? What happened?”

“There’s just been a bit of — in-fighting in the office. Nothing to be too concerned about. I just need to make sure I — don’t let my guard down again.”

“They’ve taken your name off of the door.”

“I thought they might. They do that sort of thing. Must have thought they'd killed me. But I’ll be back in there tomorrow. And I will deal with Mr King, sooner or later.”

As she stood next to the bath, Astatine realised she was seeing her for the first time without the power suit, which had been reduced to not much more than carnage-spattered rags. It was only now, seeing her stretched out and sans suit, that Astatine realised the extent of Ms Lamb's mechanisation. Her left leg was metal from the hip down, the right from just above the knee. Her torso was criss-crossed with scars and patches, some of which also had the telltale glint of artificial skin. There were wounds from injuries but also others that told more of a story; the keyhole mark of an appendectomy, the striped scar at the throat common to those who grew up on those planets with more carcinogenic atmospheres. It was a body that told a story. One day she'd get her to tell it for herself.

Ms Lamb waved at her. "Astatine?"

"Sorry."

“If you check in my bag I’ve got a med kit. Be a sweetheart and patch me up, would you?”

The bullet wound in her shoulder was a through-and-through. The head was just a graze but it had bled heavily, as head wounds tend to.

Astatine hadn’t used her sewing skills since she was young. She thought that her mother, always a bit of a revolutionary, would be surprised and probably disappointed to see her stitching up a wounded CEO. Ms Lamb, for her part, seemed not to notice the pain itself; her injuries seemed to be inconvenient, tiring more than anything else.

She pulled the thread tight, tied and cut it. The graze on her head had dried up now, the blood matting her hair into gory dreads. She helped her to shower, to clean up as well as she could without invading her personal space more than she had to. Ms Lamb sat in the bath almost like a child, the water pink around her, as Astatine shampooed her hair and gingerly rinsed the blood from her shoulders and back. When the last of the crusted blood had washed away, Astatine wrapped her in a dressing gown she’d found in a cupboard. She supported Ms Lamb as she limped out of the bathroom.

Ms Lamb headed towards the sofa, then looked across the room and frowned, puzzled. Astatine realised that she'd noticed her blanket fort.

“What’s this little… nest for?”

“Oh. Things were a bit too — spread out for me in here.”

Ms Lamb laughed.

“I should have guessed. It was probably a bit of a shock to upsize you so quickly. I just wanted to say… thank you, I suppose. So I pulled some strings. Got you the apartment of a former employee who — left suddenly, some time ago. Around the same time you joined us, in fact.”

The door clicked open. Both of them tensed, but it was only Lionel. Barring a black eye and a slight limp, he looked as per normal. Although given his quiet demeanor, he could very well be missing most of his body and not complain.

Astatine and Ms Lamb shuffled across to the sofa, sat down. Lionel sat on Ms Lamb's other side. He handed her a bottle of small orange pills and she knocked a couple back, exhaled deeply.

Then, with a flick of her finger, she switched on the TV. Astatine, who'd barely had the energy to do much beside sleep in her apartment, had been yet to find the remote.

"I have a job for you, Stat. An important one.”

“Anything.”

Ms Lamb smiled.

CHAPTER TWELVE

The screen was filled with images of what Astatine supposed was a kind of spa; not something common on their utilitarian planet.

"Every year, Automnicon has a retreat, of sorts, for its CEOs. On paper it's a relaxing time, meant for a little rest and recuperation. In practice, it's a kind of… compulsory thunderdome. Five CEOs enter, somewhat less than five leave."

"...Right."

"Over my years as one of the CEOs, I've had a good track record, which is to say, I've survived. But Mr King is new, and he's ambitious. This is only the start. He knows I'm the longest-serving CEO, so he's going after me first. And I can't let that happen.

"Security is… relatively tight, but they like to keep us on our feet, so there are always a few blind spots. Deliberate blind spots. And unlike in the office, we're somewhat limited in terms of the manpower we're allowed to bring. One bodyguard and, if applicable, one spouse. You may have met Mr King's bodyguard today. Or rather, bodyguards. They're neurally networked; apparently they count as a single person."

Astatine thought back to the blank, anaemic twins and shivered.

"However, none of my… colleagues have met you. Your internship has been under somewhat unofficial circumstances. But the tests we've put you through over the past couple of months have proved that you are capable, and your loyalty so far has been unquestionable."

"I'll do anything you need me to."

"Even if it goes against Automnicon?"

"My loyalty to you goes above my loyalty to Automnicon."

Ms Lamb smiled, rested her hand on Astatine's.

"That's what I hoped you'd say.

"Lionel is, as always, a loyal and adaptable bodyguard, but A, they know him and B, know that he runs somewhat — counter to my personal tastes. So I need you."

"You want me to act as a second bodyguard? I can do that. Of course I can do that."

'No, my sweet. I need an assassin."

CHAPTER THIRTEEN

They sat side-by-side on the sofa, going over the files on Ms Lamb's competition. They'd started with what Ms Lamb referred to as the small fry — those who likely meant her no harm.

Penelope Worthing had risen up the ranks purely through the sheer powe of her organisational skills. She was vital to the running of Automnicon and nobody would touch her if they knew what was good for them.

Likewise, Humphrey Mertdinger, one of Penelope's oldest friends, was an institution. He wasn't a kind man — nobody who possessed any kind of power within Automnicon was kind — but he was nonetheless a stable pillar of the company. And anyone who looked to lay a finger on a friend of Penelope's was likely to find the full force of her power laid down upon them, ranging from microaggressions to full decapitation. Another of thei number, an upstart from the Crab Nebula, had found that out just the yea before. Death by a thousand cuts was probably the simplest way to describ it. He'd not even made it to breakfast. All they found were his teeth. They were polished to a bright sheen and laid out neatly in order of size.

The two that Ms Lamb was targeting were the newer hires, Mr King and Mr Ambrose. Mr King, who would be bringing the twin bodyguards, was the most ambitious and therefore the most dangerous of the two. He had a background in deception and murder; he was from a business dynasty tha rivalled the Borgias. When the company faced a merger with Automnicon he was excited. When the vote didn't go his way he wiped out the rest of the boardroom then called Automnicon to report the good news.

The authorities had ruled the apparent mass suicide a cult ritual, despite the fact that most of the bodies showed signs of extreme violence and more than one had apparently hung themselves after slitting their own throat.

Mr Ambrose was more of a hobbyist when it came to murder; he liked cruelty and he liked to follow fads. His husband, to whom he was genuinely devoted, was a well-known model with a punishing daily routine. Mr Ambrose himself was a fastidious little man who was notorious for his ruthless restructuring of any company that Automnicon absorbed. He'd been the one on the phone when Mr King called to spread the good news, and the two had been firm friends ever since.

Mr Ambrose had opted for a bodyguard who was an old friend of his husband's; looking briefly into his past, the man was both unreliable and incredibly bribable, which made Astatine's job very, very simple.

Before they could get to the bloodshed, however, there was a more terrifying and awkward job to deal with; the team-building exercises.

CHAPTER FOURTEEN

She'd seen their pictures, even seen a few short videos, but Astatine still wasn't quite prepared for the characters who swept, one-by-one, into the plane. They all carried varying amounts of luggage.

The journey to the resort was uncomfortably tense but mercilessly short. Everyone was extremely, coldly polite to one another besides Humphrey and Penelope, who bunkered down in a corner of the plane and chatted over tea as if they were genuinely looking forward to the weekend that followed.

Mr King, flanked as always by the twins, whom Astatine learned were called Anya and Onaway, sat down, and Mr Ambrose followed suit, facing his ally. His husband curled up on the seat, snakelike, and the bodyguard read a book, uninterested in whatever was happening in front of him.

When everyone else was seated, Ms Lamb signalled for the pilot to take off.

They arrived fairly soon after.

The resort was a small but elegant set of buildings in the middle of nowhere. Nobody was allowed in or out barring the pilot and the CEOs; the rest of the staff lived there full time, lived out their whole lives waiting for this one yearly weekend. They were excited and terrified in turns; there was a minimum of one assassination a year during these events, and things had been heating up over the past few months.

In the middle of the resort was the main building, which was in the shape of a five-pointed star; each CEO had a suite in one of the points, with an expanse of smooth black marble and a sheer drop in between. This was, in theory, to discourage assassinations, although in practice it just encouraged a little healthy competition.

Their bags were carried in for them by eager, smartly dressed bellhops. Centipedal in nature, they carried the baggage with ease, the remainder of their limbs quietly and elegantly propelling them towards their guests' respective accommodation.

They walked into the lift, which was pentagonal, and all stood slightly awkwardly as it ascended. They passed various different floors until they reached their final destination; the top floor.

The five sides of the elevator opened, showing five different lengthy corridors. A voice spoke over the intercom.

"Please unpack. We'll see you all in an hour."

Astatine followed Ms Lamb and Lionel down the corridor. The lift doors slammed behind them with a terrifying finality.

"It's another safety measure. Stops the assassins from getting too... lazy."

Ms Lamb lead them through the door to the suite, which again had the strength and complexity of a bank vault.

This is our room. Through there is Lionel's. You can order food through here as well. There's a complicated system of dumbwaiters set up from the kitchens. Although, unfortunately, we are expected to eat all of our main meals together downstairs."

"Where should I sleep? Are we sharing, or..."

Ms Lamb looked at her, eyebrow raised. Astatine trailed off. She felt a tightness in her chest for a moment, like she was falling. There was a moment of tension between them.

"We can sort that out later. I'm going to shower. I hate planes."

CHAPTER FIFTEEN

If the CEOs of Automnicon were good at one thing, it... was not teamwork. So far they'd failed to catch one another in trust falls, Mr Ambrose had fallen right through the paper chair that was supposed to hold his weight and instead of escaping during 'the floor is lava', they'd all stood on seperate pieces of furniture and shouted at one another. It had been a long and tiring day and Astatine hadn't even started her real job yet.

Over dinner, they'd all picked at their meals (which Astatine had quickly polished off; it was possibly the most delicious thing she'd ever eaten) and made veiled, snide comments to and about one another.

And then, finally, the meal was over and their evening proper could begin.

Lionel had vanished off to his room soon after they entered the suite; Astatine wasn't sure whether he'd been told to or just decided to leave them alone. Either way, Astatine and Ms Lamb sat side-by-side on the sofa, elegant glasses of incredible expensive wine in hand.

Astatine started to speak. Then she stopped.

Ms Lamb looked at her, smiled. Tilted her head.

Ms Lamb?"

"Mhmm?"

"Why me."

"What do you mean?"

"Why did you choose me? How long were you watching me, before all of this? Why not just get someone who was a trained killer?"

"There are a lot of reasons. I wanted someone who was loyal, not only to me but also to the company. And someone who would stay by my side through whatever was thrown at us; I've only found that once before, and that was with Lionel. But, of course, on top of that I'm a romantic at heart.

"Really?"

"Well, in a way. It's hard to find someone I can trust and someone who trusts me. And has the same values.

The vast majority of Automnicon employees — voluntary employees, rather than debtors — have a problem with entitlement. They are ambitious, but only in so far as they feel that they are entitled to anything they want. They come from money, and what they want is power.

But you came from nothing and you expect nothing. And what you want isn't power, it's… I'm not even sure myself. But you aren't afraid to aim hig and you don't seem scared of doing what you have to to get there.

And this is just the start."

"You come from nothing too, right?"

She blinked. "I'm sorry?"

Astatine blushed, felt that familiar sinking feeling. "Your scars — I — "

"No." After a moment, Ms Lamb laughed. "You're right. Not that it's anyone's business but mine. I'm from a small mining town on Pluto. Freezing cold, hideously dangerous and the cultural scene of… well, a small mining town on Pluto. I did the classic small-town thing and got myself an education. Got myself a debt and set out repairing things. But then… well, some things happened. Parts of me were… lost. And I realised that it really wasn't me.

My legs were the last straw. Call me old-fashioned, but if you've lost more than half of your limbs in a job, you should probably take it as a sign and move on.

Most people… don't get to know that about me. And barring Lionel, nobody has seen me like you did in the bath. Weak. Broken. Vulnerable."

They were looking at one another intensely now, face to face, their breaths deep, almost matching.

Ms Lamb's shoulders relaxed, her face going from tight composure to a loose smile. She broke eye contact first.

"Do you want anything to eat? Room service is — "

Astatine brushed the side of her face with her hand, then leaned over and kissed her. Her lips were soft and warm, yielding. She felt a pulse rise throughout her body, from her lips right down to her toes. And then she panicked, pulled away.

"I'm — sorry. Ms Lamb. I — "

"Call me Lamb."

Ms Lamb — Lamb — pulled her in close again and they collapsed together, the priceless bottle of wine spilling into the antique rug. Lamb ran her finger along Astatine's collarbone in a way that made her shiver.

Astatine heard Lionel's door lock.

"What about the assassinations?"

"They don't usually start this early."

The pseudofur blanket on the bed was warm, almost scratchy against Astatine's back, and Ms Lamb's body was both warm and cold against hers, parts of it strangely hard and unyielding, other parts soft and inviting. They wrapped themselves up in each other as, around them, the other CEOs prepared for a long, long night.

CHAPTER SIXTEEN

Ms Lamb stretched, yawned, then nudged Astatine, who'd fallen into a warm doze.

"Okay. Time for you to go to work."

"Oh."

Ms Lamb looked across at her. "I've been planning this for a long time. I an't let — this get in the way of things."

"I…" Astatine trailed off.

Ms Lamb smiled, kissed her shoulder.

"Go on. Go kill me some colleagues. And come back safe."

Mr Ambrose was a relatively simple preposition. As Ms Lamb predicted, he had opted to sleep on this first night. His husband slept in a hyperbaric hamber to protect his skin, so he was out of the equation, and his friend — who Astatine realised was definitely under-qualified to act as a body-guard — was passed out, drunk, by the door.

She knew all this because she'd climbed across the 200 feet of smooth wall between their apartments and, perched on suction cups precariously attached to the glassy-smooth wall, was now watching the slumbering form of Mr Ambrose as he lay on the bed. His husband's chamber was pushed u beside the bed; their hands almost touching as they slept. How romantic, she thought.

Tomorrow was going to be a very unpleasant day for the other Mr Ambrose.

They all slept with their windows closed, but there was a small hole in the frame. She'd found this particular tool when browsing Automnicon's back catalogue; it was particularly unpleasant but seemed like the quickest and easiest way to do the job. An extending aerial, like one from a radio, with a razor-sharp tip. A neurotoxin on the end, lethal to the touch. And then a final element: the bleeder.

She poked it through the window, balancing the unwieldy rod as she pushed it further and further into the room. Finally it pricked the skin on the throat of the unfortunate Mr Ambrose. She pushed a little harder, saw his eyes open in shock as the needle penetrated his jugular artery. The toxi worked fast with such a short distance to travel between throat and brain; he couldn't move or shout as the tip flowered to create an unstaunchable hole. He went stiff for longer then she thought he would and then sagged, blood bubbling gently onto the pillow.

She pressed the button that detached the end and let the needle withdraw, slowly. The mattress around Mr Ambrose's head and shoulders was soaked the blood trickling steadily. The poison would hold him still, keep him frozen in position until the jugular had done its job. She watched just long enough to ensure that his death was final.

Mr King, on the other hand…

It had been a long climb round to the other side of the star, and it seemed that Mr King had brought his own traps. By the time she arrived she was already exhausted. Still, he seemed to be in bed, which wasn't quite what she'd expected. She reached through again, slid the needle through the hole. She was becoming more practiced with it now.

Mr King was sleeping on his back. At the foot of the bed, their pale bodies curled and contorted, slept the twins, catlike. She needed to ensure that she didn't strike either of them with the swinging needle, although they would be no great loss.

Eventually the needle reached the sleeping man, and she struck true, jabbing it deep into his jugular.

Nothing happened. She pressed the button, let the thing flower, but there was no gush of blood, no panic.

She tried to pull the needle back, to give it a second shot but it wouldn't come; it seemed stuck. But, she noticed, there was a little give in the window frame.

The fool had left his window unlocked.

She swore silently to herself and eased it open. She'd have to do this the hard way. But she'd been practicing.

Creeping across the floor, she could hear the twins' synchronised breathing. They breathed together, the male slightly lower pitched and the female slightly higher. She slunk past them, still holding the end of the needle aloft, and made it across to Mr King.

Or where Mr King should have been.

When she went to manually retract the needle, it was pulled out of her hands. The body in the bed was not Mr King. Whoever it was — she wasn' sure — they were still very much dead. And somebody had wedged an incredibly strong magnet into their throat.

There was a sudden absence of noise. The twins had stopped breathing. Sh span round but they were already up, rounding on her.

What she learnt, too late, was that amongst their augmentations, the twins had been granted claws. Onaway rounded on her, distracted her, as Anya launched into her from behind, sinking her claws into the side of her neck

Astatine turned, grabbed Anya by the throat, going to crush her windpipe. The woman yowled, wriggled and then, with a slash and a sickening crunch, suddenly Astatine wasn't holding her any more. She wasn't holdin anything any more.

Her hands fell to the floor with a thud, separated from the rest of her. All Astatine could do was gape at the bloody stumps. She stood shocked, frozen.

Onaway, standing beside his sister, tilted his head. Astatine's blood was splattered across his face and over the blade he'd pulled out of — somewhere. Anya reached for her, held her close, restrained her as Onaway dug the blade into her side now, jabbed at her and twisted it around like he wa stirring a pot. Then he came for her eyes with his claws.

With a swipe, Astatine was blinded. All she could hear was their hissing and all she felt was a mess of pain and numbness.

She heard Mr King emerge from — somewhere, she couldn't see where. Felt a manicured hand on her shoulder.

"Oh my. If it isn't Andrea's better half."

With a blow to her face that left her staggering, he knocked her to the ground then laid into her, kicking and crushing with his perfectly polished brogues.

"You'd think — " he punctuated each word he said with another kick " — that she — would know — to choose — someone — stronger."

When she was little more than a bloodied sack of broken bones and bruising, someone — one of the three, for they were indistinguishable now, their breath coming, synchronised, in high, excited pants — lifted her under her armpits. Her head lolled drunkenly as they heaved her across the room and onto the windowsill.

"Goodbye, little girl."

Mr King gave her a gentle shove and then she was falling, backwards, tumbling over and over, the wind rushing past her...

She was falling.

She fell.

And that was it.

CHAPTER SEVENTEEN

It was breakfast time in the shark tank. The CEOs and their entourages sat at breakfast, some seats conspicuously absent. Ms Lamb sliced a piece of parma ham into smaller and smaller pieces until, with a clang, she fractured the plate. Beside her, Lionel sat, flecks of blood forgotten on his face. Neither spoke.

Across the table, his twins on either side, Mr King was having a merry time. He shovelled forkful after forkful of fried food into his face, chewing with his mouth half open. The twins partook of anaemic pancakes, rolled tightly and eaten with little apparent joy.

"Oh, isn't your wife joining us this morning, Andrea? I suppose she was looking a little — peaky — last night."

Ms Lamb's knuckles whitened around the knife. More than anything, she wanted to hurt him, wanted to make him bleed. But there were rules. After dark was how they did their assassination.

"I do hope she feels better soon."

Screw it.

She threw the knife at him, not expecting to do any damage but hoping just to see the damn thing smack him in the face. But Anya was there, plucking the knife from midair. Her right index finger beaded with blood where she'd caught the blade.

All three of them stared at her, their heads on one side, and then raised their right hands to their mouths, sucked a finger that in only one case was bleeding.

It wasn't just his bed that Mr King was sharing with them, then.

CHAPTER EIGHTEEN

There was a click. Like someone setting a metronome going. It started slow painfully slow, then sped up until it was a strong, regular speed.

Next came a whirr. A tinny whine. An echo that went round and round.

Astatine opened her eyes.

She was lying on her back underneath a light fitting. The ceiling was a soothing shade of blue. She couldn't move, not yet.

Were these her eyes? There was something… strange about them.

Oh.

Oh, she couldn't do that before.

She squinted, focused on the light fitting and felt a slight hum as they zoomed in, refocused, zoomed in again. She read the microscopic lettering on the bulb then retracted her eyes again.

That was new.

Gingerly she sat up, feeling a strange interplay between healing muscle and new, slick metal. Everything made a noise. She assumed that, like the noises inside her biological body, she'd soon get used to it.

"They really messed you up, didn't they?"

Ms Lamb was sitting by the side of the bed. She smiled.

"Yeah." She spoke weakly. Her lungs were not quite where she expected them to be. She swallowed, feeling muscles and pistons working together in her throat.

"We had to make a lot of modifications so you'd survive. I — hope you understand."

Ms Lamb stroked her cheek, gently. As her finger drew further up her face, closer to her eye, Astatine stopped feeling the touch of her skin and instead felt the pressure of it passing over something that wasn't… her.

"You were so broken. But I knew you'd pull through. And look at what we've done for you."

Ms Lamb kissed her on the forehead and left her bedside, returning with a mirror. Astatine caught a glance at herself in the mirror and flinched, then forced herself to look again.

She was, quite frankly, a bit of a mess. What hadn't been broken in the fight had been pulverised by the fall. What skin was left was criss-crossed with seams, stitched and bandaged. Whole parts of her were missing, and there were parts that looked like they were there but were artificial now, scabbed and scarred skin stretched over intricate metal and plastic frameworks.

Both of her eyes were gone. She'd always liked her eyes, always thought they were one of her more attractive features, but they'd been replaced with things that passed for eyes but weren't — quite.

In her eye sockets were two intricate half-globed screens, both of them displaying an image of eyes. She moved the mirror, watched her fake eyes move as she looked left and right. Behind them were a series of lenses and all manner of tools, she assumed.

She could see. That was the main thing.

Her tongue was still her tongue, a little dry and bruised but still hers. Her jaw, on the other hand…

She explored the inside of her mouth with her tongue. Her new teeth were slightly cold, slightly too smooth. The notch in her right canine was gone.

The skin from the bridge of her nose to the top of her head was gone completely, replaced with an intricate series of overlapping metal panels. She frowned, raised her eyebrows and was surprised to see the panels follow her lead.

The rest of her body was a patchwork of healing and new parts. She wiggled her toes and was surprised to see her facsimiles do the same. Her torso felt peculiar, new tubes and unfamiliar shapes concealed beneath her skin. Her hands had been reattached, metal cuffs concealing the seams. She touched her fingertips together. There was still some feeling there. Hopefully, over time, she would gain more.

Ms. Lamb was smiling, but not confidently. She waited to see Astatine's reaction.

Astatine lifted her heavy arm and reached out for her. She took Ms Lamb's hand and smiled.

They wouldn't let her go now. They'd invested so much in her. She was here to stay. She'd made it.

Ms Lamb leaned over, kissed her. The kiss felt strange with her new teeth but her lips, split and battered as they were, were still the same. They kissed again, for longer this time. They held each other close.

“Good news,” she said. “You've been... promoted. Well, I suppose you’ve actually just been hired. And we've given you a new name. A codename, I suppose.

Dunnock.

Welcome to the company, sweetheart.”

Made in the USA
Monee, IL
26 May 2021